Duets for One

for Recorder
with CD play-along

Arranged by
Garth Rickard
& Heather Cox

Chester Music
(A division of Music Sales Limited)
8/9 Frith Street
London W1D 3JB

INTRODUCTION

The early stages of learning an instrument can at times be frustrating and lonely - requiring lots of practice without being able to join an ensemble and enjoy playing with other musicians.

We put this book together to give recorder players at the earliest stages the opportunity to have more fun - playing duets with great backing tracks whilst gaining all the benefits of ensemble playing.

All the tunes are popular and many you will know already. Listen to the complete performances on the CD with both recorders (tracks 2 - 17) to learn each piece; you may find it helps to practise by playing along with these parts.

Then you can select a part to play on your own with the CD by moving on to tracks 18 - 49. Once you have learnt one part, then you can move on to the other. The easiest parts are suitable for pre-grade one players, but the incentive to learn the melodies mean that you will soon be able to move on to the top part!

Alternatively, you can simply play these easy duets with a friend. However you decide to use this book, we hope you will have lots of fun whilst improving your recorder playing.

Heather Cox and Garth Rickard

This book © Copyright 2001 Chester Music
Order No. CH62865 ISBN 0-7119-9013-1

Solo recorder: Heather Cox
Music processed by Enigma Music Production Services
Cover design by Ian Butterworth
Printed in Great Britain by Printwise (Haverhill) Limited, Suffolk

CONTENTS

Morning Has Broken

This melody has been popular since the early 70's, when Cat Stevens made it a hit.
You will find the harmony part very easy.

Traditional

The Water Is Wide

In this English folk song you will find the
harmony part simple to play. It uses just four notes.

Traditional

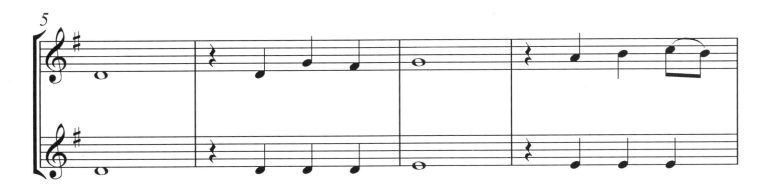

(pause on last time only)

Heartbeat

This Buddy Holly hit has become popular
again through the T.V. series 'Heartbeat'.

Words & Music by
Bob Montgomery & Norman Petty

Freight Train

Listen out for the pedal steel guitar in this American country song.

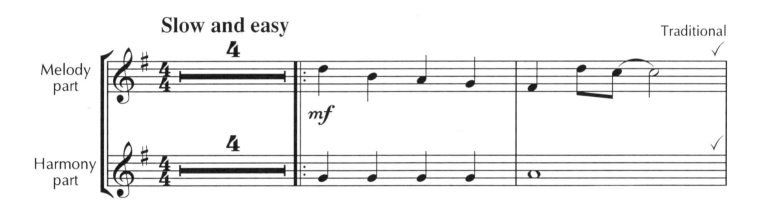

Funky Twinkle

This funky arrangement of a well-known tune uses a syncopated rhythm.
Listen to it before playing – it's much easier than it looks!

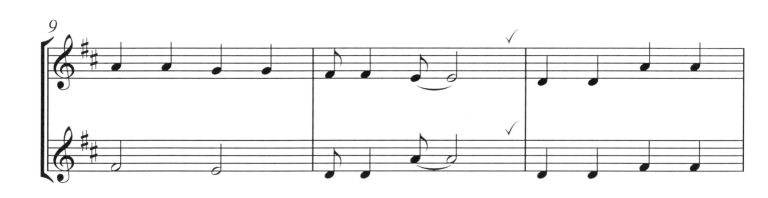

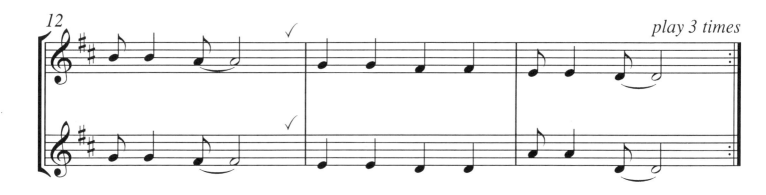

Cherry Ripe

In this English folk song you play as part of a quartet.
There are two recorders, cello and piano.

With elegance

Traditional

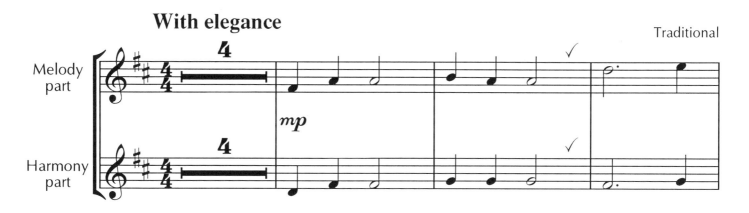

Words

The Bee Gees wrote and had a hit with this song originally.
It was recently re-recorded by Boyzone.

Words & music by
Barry Gibb, Robin Gibb and Maurice Gibb

I Never Will Marry

You will hear on the CD that the harmony part doesn't play the first time through.
The melody is easy – you could try it first.

Traditional

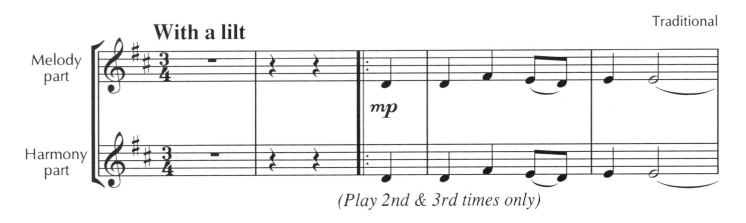

(Play 2nd & 3rd times only)

The Banks Of The Ohio

Listen out for the key change! The whole tune moves up a tone from G to A.
Musicians often do this, towards the end of a piece, to give it a 'lift'.

Laid back

Traditional

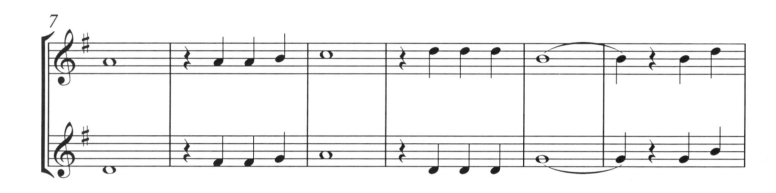

Pachelbel's Canon

This harmony part is eight notes played over and over. Listen out for the other instruments joining in and building up the piece on the CD.

Gentle and steady

By Johann Pachelbel

Any Dream Will Do

This song is from 'Joseph And The Amazing Technicolour® Dreamcoat', and was recorded by Jason Donovan.

Music by Andrew Lloyd Webber
Lyrics by Tim Rice

Dona Nobis Pacem

This piece of music has an organ accompaniment on the CD.
Listen out for the angelic choir!

Gracefully

Traditional

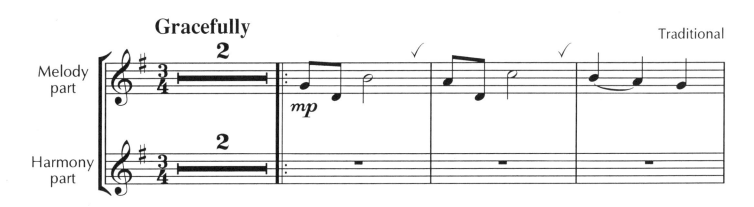

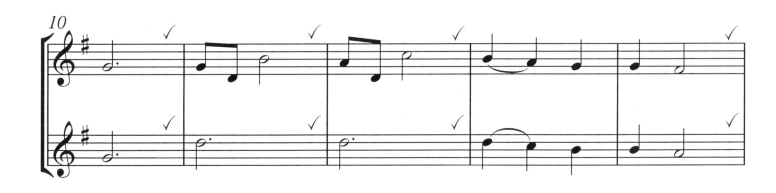

rit. (last time only)

Pick A Bale O' Cotton

The quick notes will be easy if you relax, chew on a piece of straw, and enjoy the tune!
The harmony part is very simple – just three notes.

The Steamboat

In this Dutch folk song the harmony part plays above and below the melody.

Happily

Traditional

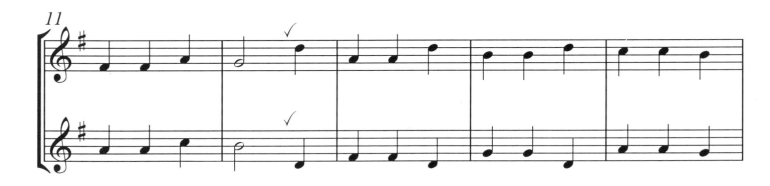

Scarborough Fair

This old English folk song was made famous by Simon and Garfunkel.

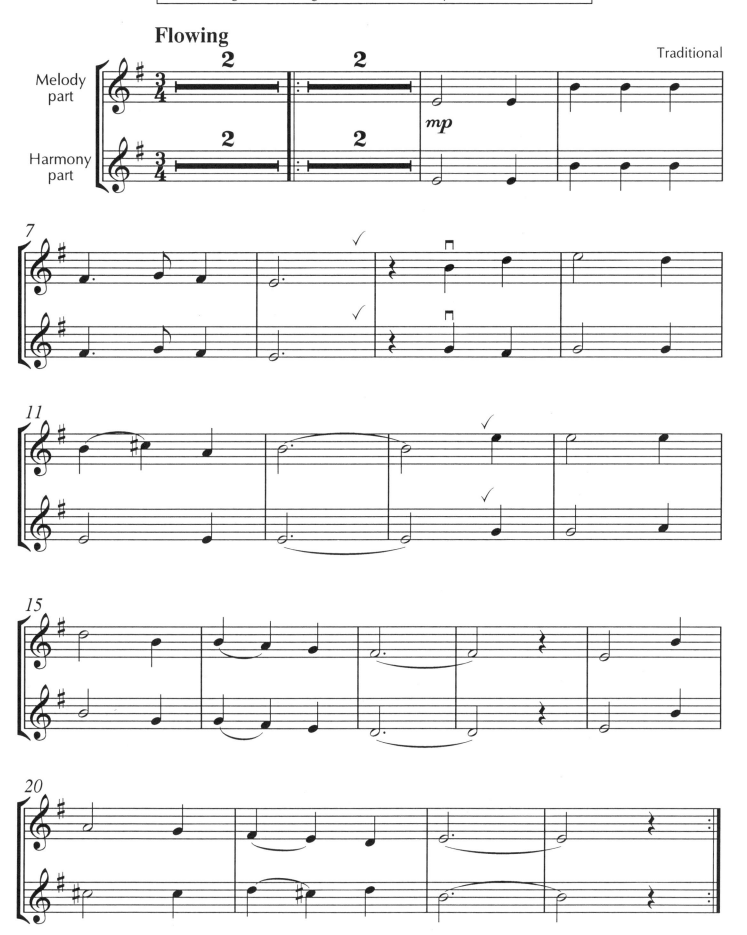

Killing Me Softly With His Song

This song was recently re-recorded by The Fugees.
If you find the rhythms difficult, listen to the performance on the CD before playing.

Words by Norman Gimbel
Music by Charles Fox

TRACK LISTING

1   Tuning Note (Concert A)

Complete performances:

2   **Morning Has Broken**
(Traditional) Chester Music Ltd

3   **The Water Is Wide**
(Traditional) Chester Music Ltd

4   **Heartbeat**
(Montgomery/Petty) Peermusic (UK) Ltd

5   **Freight Train**
(Traditional) Chester Music Ltd

6   **Funky Twinkle**
(Traditional) Chester Music Ltd

7   **Cherry Ripe**
(Traditional) Chester Music Ltd

8   **Words**
(Gibb/Gibb/Gibb) BMG Music Publishing Ltd

9   **I Will Never Marry**
(Traditional) Chester Music Ltd

10 **Banks Of The Ohio**
(Traditional) Chester Music Ltd

11 **Pachelbel's Canon**
(Pachelbel) Chester Music Ltd

12 **Any Dream Will Do**
(Lloyd Webber/Rice) The Really Useful Group Ltd

13 **Dona Nobis Pacem**
(Traditional) Chester Music Ltd

14 **Pick A Bale O' Cotton**
(Traditional) Chester Music Ltd

15 **The Steamboat**
(Traditional) Chester Music Ltd

16 **Scarborough Fair**
(Traditional) Chester Music Ltd

17 **Killing Me Softly With His Song**
(Gimbel/Fox) Onward Music Ltd

Melody part with backing tracks:

18 **Morning Has Broken**
19 **The Water Is Wide**
20 **Heartbeat**
21 **Freight Train**
22 **Funky Twinkle**
23 **Cherry Ripe**
24 **Words**
25 **I Will Never Marry**
26 **Banks Of The Ohio**
27 **Pachelbel's Canon**
28 **Any Dream Will Do**
29 **Dona Nobis Pacem**
30 **Pick A Bale O' Cotton**
31 **The Steamboat**
32 **Scarborough Fair**
33 **Killing Me Softly With His Song**

Harmony part with backing tracks:

34 **Morning Has Broken**
35 **The Water Is Wide**
36 **Heartbeat**
37 **Freight Train**
38 **Funky Twinkle**
39 **Cherry Ripe**
40 **Words**
41 **I Will Never Marry**
42 **Banks Of The Ohio**
43 **Pachelbel's Canon**
44 **Any Dream Will Do**
45 **Dona Nobis Pacem**
46 **Pick A Bale O' Cotton**
47 **The Steamboat**
48 **Scarborough Fair**
49 **Killing Me Softly With His Song**